Destiny
the Rock Star
Fairy

To Emilia, with love

Special thanks to Rachel Elliot

ISBN 978-0-545-27056-4

17 16 15 14   16/0

Printed in the U.S.A.   40
First Scholastic printing, September 2011

Destiny
the Rock Star
Fairy

by Daisy Meadows

SCHOLASTIC INC.

New York   Toronto   London   Auckland

Sydney   Mexico City   New Delhi   Hong Kong

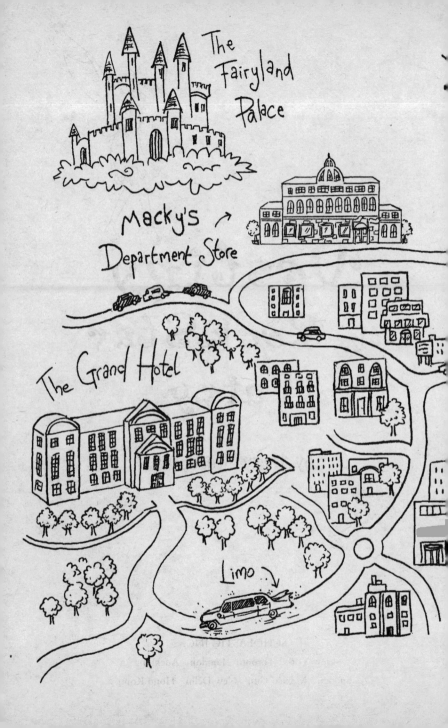

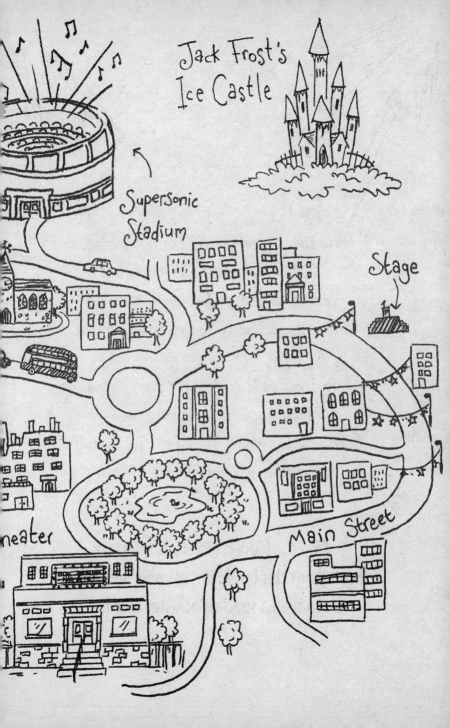

I'm sick of songs, and I'm not joking.
Turn all singing into croaking!
Costumes tear and dancers stumble.
Make the audience groan and grumble.

To spoil each rock star's starry glee,
Take the fairy's objects three.
Hide them where they can't be found,
And silence every pretty sound!

**Find the hidden letters in the stars
throughout this book. Unscramble all 7 letters
to spell a special rock star word!**

The Sparkly
Sash

Contents

Christmas Angels

"I can't believe that we're really going to meet Serena, Emilia, and Lexy!" Kirsty Tate said for the hundredth time that day.

"Neither can I!" agreed her best friend Rachel Walker.

Kirsty squeezed Rachel's hand as they stood in the entrance to their hotel suite with their parents. The girls had won a competition to meet their favorite girl

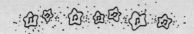

group, The Angels. They were staying
overnight in The Grand Hotel. They
were going to get a makeover from the
band's stylists, help the band turn on
the city's Christmas lights, and go to
The Angels' Christmas charity concert
tomorrow night!

"This is going to be almost as exciting
as one of our fairy
adventures!"
Kirsty whispered
to her best friend.
No one else
knew that they
had a special
friendship with the
king and queen of
Fairyland. Kirsty and Rachel had gone
on many adventures with the fairies as

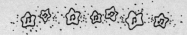

they tried to stop Jack Frost and his goblins from making mischief.

"This hotel reminds me of the palace in Fairyland!" said Rachel, looking around their room with wide eyes. "It's so beautiful!"

"Oh, Rachel, look!" cried Kirsty. On a table in a corner of their room was the largest bunch of flowers the girls had ever seen, with a handwritten card on top.

Dear Kirsty and Rachel,

We hope you have a fun stay! We are really looking forward to meeting you later today. Serena, Emilia, & Lexy
— The Angels xxx

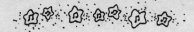

While their parents unpacked, Kirsty and Rachel explored the enormous hotel suite. Their favorite room was the lounge. It was covered with red and gold Christmas decorations. In the middle of the room was a huge Christmas tree that filled their noses with the scent of pine.

"Oh, Kirsty! Look at the tiny bells hanging from the branches!" cried Rachel.

4

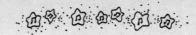

As she spoke, the tree seemed to shiver and the little bells tinkled. A burst of gold glitter cascaded down from the angel on top of the tree like a sparkling waterfall. When the whirl of glitter stopped, the girls saw a beautiful fairy sitting on a piece of red tinsel, waving at them. "Hello," she said in a musical voice. "I'm Destiny the Rock Star Fairy." "It's wonderful to meet you!" exclaimed Kirsty.

"Thank you!" said Destiny with a
dazzling smile. "It's great to meet
you both, too. I've heard so
much about you
from King
Oberon and
Queen
Titania!"

"What are
you doing in the
city?" Rachel asked.
"We're here because
we won a contest to meet
the Angels."

"I know all about the competition,"
Destiny said. "That's why I'm here,
too!"

"What do you mean?" asked
Rachel.

"I need your help," Destiny said, her smile fading. "I look after all the rock stars in the human world, and I'm a singer in Fairyland, too. Every year, we have a big Christmas concert in Fairyland. There's music and dancing and spectacular performances from some of the fairies. At the end, I always do a rock show. But now we may have to cancel the whole concert!"

"Oh, no!" cried the girls. "Why?"

"Jack Frost decided that he wanted to perform the big closing number with his group," Destiny explained.

"Frosty and his
Gobolicious Band?"
cried Rachel. "But
they're terrible!"

Rachel
remembered how
Jack Frost and his
band had once tried to win the
National Talent Competition. He had
stolen the Music Fairies' magic musical
instruments, so that nobody could play
their music correctly and his band would
sound the best. The girls and the Music
Fairies had managed to stop him just in
time.

"Jack Frost still thinks that he's the best
singer in all of Fairyland," Destiny said.
"He demanded top billing in the show."

"What did you do?" asked Kirsty.

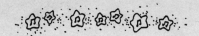

"We let him audition," said Destiny, "but his singing and the band's playing was so awful that we just couldn't say yes. I told him to practice and audition again next year, but he lost his temper. He said that if he couldn't be the star of the show, he would get rid of all rock music entirely!"

Jack Frost's Revenge

Rachel and Kirsty could hardly believe their ears.

"But how could Jack Frost get rid of all rock music?" Kirsty asked.

Destiny's shoulders sagged.

"I have three magic objects that are very important to Fairyland and to the human world," she said. "The sparkly sash protects rock stars' costumes. The harmony key protects their music, and the magic microphone ensures that the sound and lighting systems work smoothly. But Jack Frost has stolen all three magic objects." Destiny sighed. "He's instructed his goblins to hide them here in the city in order to ruin our Fairyland concert. He also wants to make trouble for The Angels' Christmas charity concert at the same time, since they're the most popular rock group in the country!"

"So while the magic objects are missing, things are going to go wrong for music groups in the human

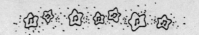

world?" Rachel asked.

Destiny nodded sadly.

"We can't let the charity concert be ruined," said Kirsty in a determined voice. "We have to get the magic objects back before tomorrow night!"

"That means you'll help me?" asked Destiny.

"Of course!" said Rachel and Kirsty together.

"I hoped you were going to say that!" said Destiny with a big smile. "When

I heard that you'd won the contest, I realized that you would be in exactly the right place to help me."

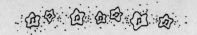

"What do you want us to do?" asked Rachel eagerly.

"For now, just stay alert," said Destiny. "The goblins are somewhere in the city and they're sure to cause trouble sooner or later."

"We won't let those awful goblins get away with their plans," Rachel declared.

"Remember, keep a close eye on The Angels," Destiny added. "Jack Frost definitely wants to ruin things for them."

The girls nodded, and Destiny disappeared with another burst of gold glitter. Before the girls could speak, Mrs.

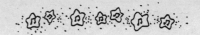

Tate came in to say that it was time to go to the stadium and meet The Angels. At that moment, all other thoughts flew out of Rachel's and Kirsty's minds. They were about to meet their favorite rock stars!

Mrs. Walker and Mrs. Tate rode in the limousine with Rachel and Kirsty, while their dads stayed behind at the hotel. When they reached the stadium, they went to the backstage door. There they were met by a man with a clipboard and a headset who smiled and waved.

"Welcome to the Supersonic Stadium!" he said. "I'm here to take you to meet The Angels."

He led the girls and their moms though the backstage door and down a long hallway lined with dressing rooms. The last door had a gold star with two familiar names printed on it.

RACHEL WALKER & KIRSTY TATE

When the girls pushed open the door, they heard a trio of excited squeals. All three of The Angels grinned and rushed over to hug them. The members of the band were even prettier in real life than they looked on TV!

Emilia was tall and graceful, with big green eyes and straight blond hair that swished around her face. She was wearing a pair of blue skinny jeans and a dark red sweater over a sparkling camisole.

Serena had silky black hair and beautiful brown eyes. She was wearing

teal leggings and a fitted shirt in
swirling blues and browns, with a wide
belt that sat loosely on her hips.

Lexy's sparkling blue eyes were full of
fun. She had curly strawberry blond hair
that flowed down her back, and she was
wearing a green dress with knee-high
tan boots.

"Welcome!" cried Emilia.

"Congratulations on winning the
contest," said Serena with a smile.

"It's great to meet you!" Lexy

added, her ringlets bouncing.

Mrs. Tate and Mrs. Walker left to get a cup of coffee, and The Angels told Rachel and Kirsty their plan for the day.

"You're going to get star treatment from our own stylists," Emilia began.

"Then we'll give you a tour around the stadium," Serena added.

"But *first*, we're going to teach you the dance routine for our brand-new song!" Lexy finished eagerly.

The Glitter Trail

Half an hour later, Rachel and Kirsty were giggling with The Angels like old friends as they learned the dance steps.

"We did it!" Rachel cheered at last. "We got all the way through with no mistakes!"

They hugged as the door opened and a man and woman walked in.

"Girls, this is Rich and Charlotte,
our stylist and our makeup artist,"
said Emilia. "Rich can tell you what
colors and styles look good on you, and
Charlotte will do your makeup!"

"Makeup should be simple and pretty,"
Charlotte said, pulling out a tube of
sparkling lip gloss
and a pot of
silvery glitter.

The girls sat
down in front of
a mirror. As
Charlotte
dabbed glitter
on their cheeks and eyelids, Rich talked
about the colors and styles that would be
flattering on them. The Angels watched
and chatted happily.

When Charlotte was done, the girls went over to look at themselves in the full-length mirror on the back of the dressing-room door. Suddenly, Emilia's cell phone started to ring. As soon as she answered it, her face fell.

"But this could ruin the whole show!" she cried.

Rachel and Kirsty exchanged worried glances.

"That was our agent, Robin," Emilia said as she hung up. "The truck carrying our costumes is missing! Robin can't reach the driver on his cell phone, and she has no idea where he is."

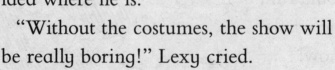

"Without the costumes, the show will be really boring!" Lexy cried.

"That's terrible," Kirsty said to Rachel.

"This must have happened because Jack Frost has Destiny's sash," Rachel murmured.

Just then, Rachel and
Kirsty heard the
sound of running
footsteps in
the hallway
and a familiar,
squawking
giggle.

"That sounds
like goblins!" Kirsty
whispered urgently to Rachel. "I bet
they have the sparkly sash with them!"

Rich, Charlotte, and The Angels were
all talking at once, and they weren't
paying attention to the girls. It was a
perfect chance to escape!

"Let's go see if we can find the goblins
while they're busy talking," Rachel
whispered.

The girls slipped out of the dressing room. Just down the hallway, a door was standing wide open.

"It looks like a storage room," said Kirsty, stepping inside. "Oh, no!"

The girls stared in horror. The room was a complete mess. Containers of face powder had been dumped out, dusting everything in a fine layer of pinks and bronzes. Empty tubes of cream eye shadow littered the floor, and the shimmering

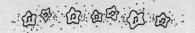

costumes on the clothes rack
were smeared with purple,
blue, and gold. Face
glitter was
rubbed on the
walls and
ground into
the carpet.
"Look at this!"
said Rachel.
Someone had
used red lipstick to
draw a picture of Jack
Frost on the wall with his tongue
sticking out!

"This is definitely the work of
goblins!" said Kirsty angrily.

Suddenly, Rachel grabbed Kirsty's arm.

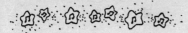

"I think something's still in here!" she hissed, pointing into the far corner.

A long, silver boot was wiggling around on the floor. It was much too small to hide a goblin, but *something* was definitely inside it!

"What is it?" cried Kirsty, stepping backward.

The boot shook again, and a jet of gold glitter shot out of the top. Then Destiny appeared right in front of Rachel and Kirsty!

"Hi, girls!" said the little fairy,

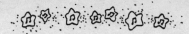

looking dismayed by the mess in the room. "What happened here?"

"It's the goblins," said Kirsty. "They're in the stadium! And the truck full of The Angels' costumes has disappeared."

"Then we need to find the goblins quickly," said Destiny with a frown. "They must have my sparkly sash."

She waved her wand, and there was a flurry of magic sparkles. When they cleared, the room was clean and tidy again.

"Let's go find the sparkly sash before the goblins cause any more trouble!" Destiny said.

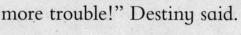

She tucked herself into Kirsty's pocket, and the girls hurried out into the hallway.

"Look!" cried Rachel, pointing at a trail of messy footprints on the floor. "These should lead us straight to the goblins!"

They followed the footprints along the hallway and through three sets of double

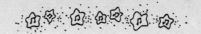

doors. At last, they arrived at the back
of the main stage.

Wires and cords trailed across the
floor, and panels of switches were
everywhere. Temporary steps led up to
an archway, which was the entrance to
the stage.

"Listen!" said Rachel softly.

There were horrible screeching sounds
coming from the stage. On tiptoe, Kirsty
made her way up the steps, motioning
for Rachel to follow her. Slowly they
crept up the stairs and peered down at
the stage.

Transparent steps led down to the
main stage area, which was crowded
with large floodlights, tall microphone
stands . . . and five goblins prancing
around the stage!

Showtime!

Kirsty and Rachel had to clap their
hands over their mouths to stop
themselves from laughing out loud.
The goblins had raided the storage closet
and tried to dress up like rock stars!

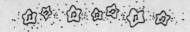

One goblin had a lime green feather boa wrapped around his body. Another goblin was wearing a thick layer of bright pink blush and had scarlet lipstick smeared all around his mouth. The other goblins were wearing silky shirts and sparkling shorts. One of them was twirling a long, clip-on hair extension that he had attached to his bony head.

They were singing into microphones . . . or *trying* to sing.

"That's the worst noise I've ever

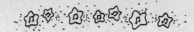

heard!" cried Destiny, putting her hands over her ears. "Thank goodness the microphones aren't turned on!"

"Look!" Kirsty exclaimed. The smallest goblin had something wrapped around his waist— something long and gold that shimmered and glimmered in the stage lights. "It's the sparkly sash!" Destiny exclaimed. "How are we going to get it away from the goblin?" Rachel asked.

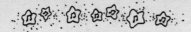

Suddenly, Kirsty smiled.

"I've got an idea!" she said. "Rachel, do you remember the dance routine that The Angels taught us?"

"I think so," Rachel said, nodding.

"Let's go teach it to the goblins," Kirsty suggested, her eyes shining. "While they're concentrating on the steps, Destiny can take the sash!"

"That just might work!" Rachel

declared. "They'll all have to face the same direction and stay in one place. Then Destiny can fly up behind them without being seen!"

Rachel and Kirsty climbed down the steps and stood at the stage entrance.

"Hi!" called Kirsty. "You must be the backup dancers. We're going to show you the new routine!"

One of the goblins giggled and nudged the others.

"They think we're humans!" he

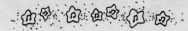

whispered loudly. "Our awesome disguises have fooled them!"

The girls began to walk the goblins through the routine. They were *very* clumsy. *Crash!* They turned the wrong way and banged into each other. *Bump!* They stepped on each other's toes and hopped around, squealing. *Clang!* They tripped over wires and

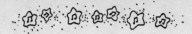

knocked down all the microphone
stands.

In the middle of the chaos, Destiny
fluttered up behind the smallest goblin.
As he pranced to the left and then to
the right, the fairy flew closer and
closer. Rachel and Kirsty both held their
breath. Could Destiny get the sash back
before she was spotted?

Seizing the Sash

"Side-together-side, and reach for the stars!" Kirsty chanted.

The goblin wearing the sparkly sash was concentrating so hard, his tongue was sticking out. He kept shaking his hips from side to side, and Destiny couldn't untie the sash.

"Keep your hips nice and still!" called Rachel.

Destiny gave Rachel a grateful wink
and began to loosen the sparkly sash
with her fingers. Slowly and gently,
the little fairy
slipped the sash
away from the
goblin's waist.
At last, it fell
into her hands,
and she returned
it to its fairy
size as she
flitted away!

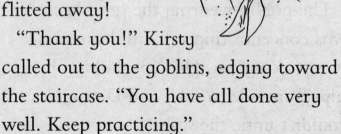

"Thank you!" Kirsty
called out to the goblins, edging toward
the staircase. "You have all done very
well. Keep practicing."

As they ran up the steps, the smallest
goblin gave a furious yell.

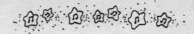

"My sash!" he shrieked, pointing a bony finger at the girls. "Thieves! They stole my sash!"

The girls froze on the staircase and Destiny flew over to join them, carrying the precious sash.

"*You* are the thieves!" she told the goblins. "I'm going to return the sparkly sash to Fairyland, where it belongs!"

"We won't let you ruin The Angels' Christmas concert," Rachel added bravely.

"Catch them!" squawked the goblin wearing a bow.

The goblins rushed toward the girls.

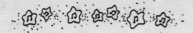

"Oh, no you don't!" Destiny declared.
She waved her wand and a cloud of
fairy dust surrounded the girls. As they
blinked, they felt themselves becoming
as small as Destiny. Fine, pretty wings
appeared on their backs. Fluttering them
delightedly, the girls rose into the air
as the goblins charged at them from all
directions.

THUMP! The
goblins bumped into
each other and fell to
the ground, screeching
with rage. They immediately
got back up and sprang
into the air, trying to reach
the girls, who were
hovering just out of reach.

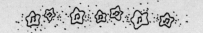

Because their eyes were on the girls, they weren't looking where they were going. They ran blindly into each other, yelling as they knocked each other down and stumbled over the lights and other equipment on stage!

Destiny clapped her hands to get the goblins' attention. "You'd better go tell

Jack Frost that you don't have the sash anymore," she said. "I wouldn't want to be in your shoes when he hears that I have it back!" The goblins looked sadly at each other, and shuffled off toward the exit.

"Now I should clean up this mess," Destiny said. With a wave of her wand and a little fairy magic, the stage was soon back to normal.

Rachel, Kirsty, and Destiny flew back to the hallway and into the storage room. Destiny was still holding the precious sparkly sash.

"Thank you so much for your help, girls," Destiny said, happily clutching the sash to her chest. "I could never have gotten this back without you."

They all hugged, and then Destiny waved her wand again and returned Rachel and Kirsty to their human size.

"Are you going to take the sash back

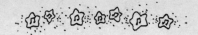

to Fairyland now?" asked Kirsty.

Destiny nodded.

"The sooner it's back in its rightful place, the better!" she declared. "Good-bye, girls. I'll see you again soon!"

Rachel and Kirsty waved as Destiny disappeared in a whirl of sparkles. Then Rachel squeezed Kirsty's hand.

"Come on!" she said. "Let's get back to The Angels!"

In the dressing room, Rachel and Kirsty found The Angels hugging and jumping around with excitement. Lexy saw the girls and rushed over to them.

"They found the truck!" she squealed happily, dancing around the room. "The driver's GPS sent him to a duck farm in the middle of the countryside! Then his truck broke down and he couldn't call us because his cell phone battery was dead. But at the last minute, a tow truck drove past

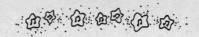

and rescued him, and then his GPS
started working again. Can you believe
it?"

"The costumes are all safe," said
Emilia. "So now we can relax and
give you that tour of the stadium we
promised. Come on, girls!"

As they started out, Rachel and Kirsty
shared a secret smile. The sash was back
in Fairyland, and costumes everywhere
were safe! Now there were only two
magic objects left to find.

"Isn't it amazing that the truck was
found so quickly?" said Serena, linking
arms with the girls as they walked into
the hallway.

Kirsty and Rachel looked at each
other and giggled.

"It's just like magic!" said Kirsty.

The Harmony Key

Contents

Shopping Like Stars

At breakfast the next morning, Mr. Tate had a surprise for the girls.

"We thought you would like some new outfits to wear to the concert tonight, so we're taking you shopping at Macky's," he said.

"That's the biggest department store in the whole city!" gasped Rachel, her eyes sparkling. "That's so exciting! We'll be able to use the tips Rich gave us."

But when the adults started talking about how to get to Macky's, Kirsty whispered in Rachel's ear.

"What about the harmony key?" she asked. "I really want to visit Macky's, but we have to help Destiny get her other two magic objects back before Jack Frost and his goblins ruin rock music forever!"

"Queen Titania always says that we should let the magic come to us," Rachel said thoughtfully. "I think we should go to Macky's, but keep a lookout for anything that might lead us to the goblins and the harmony key."

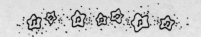

"You're right," Kirsty said. "Oh Rachel, I can't wait to see what Macky's is really like!"

The Macky's building was truly magnificent. It was made of gleaming white marble and was surrounded by big pillars. Flags fluttered above every entrance, and tall doormen in blue uniforms held the heavy glass doors open for the girls and their parents.

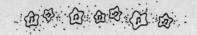

Rachel and Kirsty felt very excited as they rode up the long escalators to the third floor. The juniors department was huge! As their parents headed off in one direction, Rachel and Kirsty hurried eagerly toward a rack that was full of clothes in all the colors of the rainbow.

Kirsty pulled out a pretty red skirt and a fitted white top with a sparkly red star on the front. "This would look great with some glittery ballet flats!" she said.

Suddenly, a small child ran past them

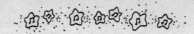

and pushed
Rachel into the
clothing rack.
"Hey!' cried Kirsty.
"You should be
more careful!"
But the child didn't
respond. He or she
was wearing a hooded sweatshirt, and
ran over to join two other children.
They began pushing each other and
yelling.

"I'm OK," said Rachel, turning back
to look at the clothes again. "That skirt
is just right, Kirsty. It's red—the color
that Rich and Charlotte said looks the
best on you. You should try it on!"

"First we have to find something for

you to try on, too!" said Kirsty with a
smile. "Rich said that blue would look
great on you."

They looked through the racks, pulling
out clothes and holding them up against
each other. Suddenly Kirsty gave an
excited cry.

"Perfect!" she said triumphantly.

She had found a pair of dark blue
jeans with sequin trim on the back
pockets and the waistband, and a bright
blue wrap top covered
in tiny sequins and
sparkles. Rachel
clapped her hands
together.

"Amazing!" she
declared. "Kirsty,
I think you're as

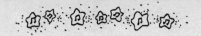

good a stylist as Rich!"

Just then, there was a loud shout from the dress department. The rowdy kids Rachel and Kirsty had seen earlier were now parading around the store in expensive evening dresses. Their heads were draped in silky scarves, and one of them had just stepped on another's gown.

"What noisy children!" said Mr. Tate, walking up behind the girls. "I wonder where their parents are."

"I haven't seen any grown-ups with them," commented Rachel.

"Hmm, it's strange to see so many little kids running around on their own like that," said Kirsty thoughtfully.

"Ah, I see you've found some outfits," said Mrs. Walker.

"You'd better try them on," said Mrs. Tate.

The best friends walked into the dressing room and chose an empty stall. As they tried on their new outfits, Kirsty leaned closer to Rachel.

"I think those kids we saw might actually be goblins!" she said in a whisper. "They keep hiding their faces,

they're the right size, and there are no
adults with them."

Rachel nodded in agreement.

"We need to find out what they're
up to," she said. "But we can't follow
them—our parents are waiting right
outside!"

They stood side by side and looked
into the large mirror. The clothes looked
great, but now they had even more
important things to think about!

"Let's tell our parents that we like these outfits, and then we'll try to get closer to the goblins," said Kirsty. "They're bound to be carrying the harmony key with them."

Rachel nodded, and they changed into their own clothes again. Kirsty bent down to tie her shoelace . . . and froze.

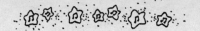

Very slowly, she looked up at Rachel
and gestured for her to come take a
look. As Rachel bent down, Kirsty
pointed.

Poking out from the bottom of the
stall next-door was a pair of large,
green feet!

Goblin Fashion

"Now that is definitely a goblin!" Rachel hissed.

"Absolutely," agreed Kirsty in a low voice. "Come on!"

The girls stepped out of their dressing room and Kirsty pulled open the curtain of the one next to them.

The goblin inside didn't notice them at first. He was too busy admiring himself in the full-length mirror! He was wearing a purple velvet suit and a rainbow-striped vest. As they watched, he raised a fedora to his head.

Kirsty and Rachel burst out laughing at the sight of the vain goblin! He whirled around and let out an embarrassed yelp of surprise. His green cheeks went red.

"You terrible girls!" he stammered.

"How dare you laugh at me! I'm the most fashionable goblin in the whole world!"

He stuck out his tongue and darted past them angrily.

"Quick," said Kirsty, trying to stop giggling. "We have to follow him!"

The girls dashed after the goblin, but they ran straight into their parents, who had been waiting outside the dressing rooms on cushy sofas.

"So, did you like the outfits?" asked Mrs. Walker.

"We loved them," said Rachel.

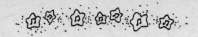

"Wonderful!" said Mrs. Tate. "Let's go look for shoes to match."

Kirsty and Rachel exchanged desperate glances as the well-dressed goblin disappeared behind a clothing display. They would have to give up the chase . . . for now.

The shoe department was up on the next floor. As the girls and their parents rode up the escalator, Rachel and Kirsty spotted three small figures dressed in bright clothes and wearing long wigs. One had bouncing black ringlets, another had sleek blond locks, and the third had fiery red hair. They

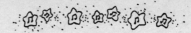

were running up the down escalator, shrieking with laughter. Shoppers were leaping out of their way and pressing themselves against the side of the escalator to avoid them.

Suddenly, the black-haired goblin fell over the side of the escalator onto the one going the other way. He started to wail as he rode up the escalator away from his friends.

"Jump off!" shouted the blond goblin, riding down to the bottom and staring up.

"No, stay on and then come down the other way!" shouted the redhead, joining him.

The black-haired goblin began to
run down the up escalator, puffing and
panting, while the other two shouted
words of encouragement.

"You can do it!"

"Faster!"

He put on an extra burst of speed, lost his balance, and tumbled head over heels to the bottom of the escalator. He landed at the feet of an angry-looking security guard in a blue and silver uniform.

"What's going on here?" the security guard demanded.

"Run away!" shrieked the blond goblin.

The goblins scattered, and the security guard chased after them. They made a break for the music department.

"We have to follow them!" whispered

Kirsty to Rachel. The girls chose their new shoes very quickly, and a few minutes later they were lining up to pay.

"After all that shopping, I could use a cup of coffee," said Mr. Tate. "Would anyone be interested in going to the café on the top floor?"

"Good idea!" said the other adults.

"I'm not thirsty," Rachel said. "Are you, Kirsty? If not, maybe we could go and look around the music department instead?"

"That sounds fine," said Mrs. Walker. "We'll meet you in the café when

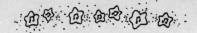

you're done looking around."

"Come on," said Kirsty in a low voice, as she and Rachel headed away from the adults. "We have to stop those goblins from causing any more trouble—and find out if they have the harmony key!"

"Look at that mirror!" said Rachel suddenly.

She pointed to a mirror by a shelf of shoes. They had been using it to see the shoes they were trying on. But now it

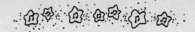

wasn't reflecting the girls' feet. It was shimmering and sparkling with gold and red light!

"Oh, Rachel," whispered Kirsty. "It's fairy magic!"

The Missing Music

The girls dropped to their knees next to the mirror. It began to ripple like water after a pebble has been thrown into it. Rachel and Kirsty caught a glimpse of pink towers and blue sky. Then a small figure filled the mirror and burst out of it in a flurry of golden sparkles and music notes. It was Destiny!

"Hello, girls!" she said. "Any sign of the harmony key?"

"Destiny, it's great to see you!" Rachel smiled.

"You're just in time," Kirsty added. "The goblins are here in Macky's, and they're causing lots of trouble!"

"We were about to follow them to the music department," said Rachel. "But it's hard to keep them in sight."

"Well, let's see what we can do about that," said Destiny with a smile.

She waved her wand. With a flurry of fairy dust, the girls shrunk to fairy size, complete with glittering, gauzy wings.

"Thank you!" said Rachel, fluttering

her delicate wings
and doing a
somersault in the
air. "They won't
spot us so easily
now!"

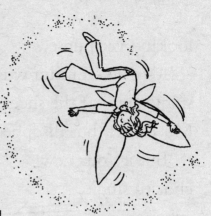

"This way!" said
Destiny, pointing toward the next
department. "I have something to show
you, and the electronics department is the
perfect place to do it."

They fluttered toward the electronics
department, making sure the other
shoppers didn't see them. Destiny waved
her wand at a row of flickering TV
screens in front. A golden crackle
erupted on the screens, and an image
of The Angels appeared on every one.
They were in their dressing room,

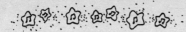

looking very upset.

"It's true," Emilia was saying. "Every single copy of the sheet music for 'Key to My Heart' has disappeared!"

"But it's our new charity single," groaned Serena. "We have to sing it at the concert tonight, or nobody will buy it—then the charity won't get any money."

"Without the sheet music, none of the backup singers and musicians will be able to perform,"

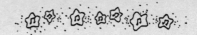

said Lexy. "What are we going to do?"

The images faded, and Destiny looked sadly at Rachel and Kirsty.

"This isn't a coincidence," she said. "The harmony key protects rock stars' music. Without it, everything could go wrong for The Angels . . . and their favorite charity won't get a cent!"

"We're not going to let Jack Frost ruin everything," said Kirsty in a determined voice. "Come on, let's find those goblins and *make* them give back the harmony key!"

Hide and
Seek

When the girls reached the music
department, everything seemed calm
and quiet.

"Maybe they've gone to another
department," Kirsty suggested.

"No, listen!" said Rachel.

The girls could hear a rhythmic
squeaking sound in the distance. It grew
louder and louder, until a unicycle with
a squeaky wheel sped around the corner,
ridden by a goblin wearing a long dress.
Close behind him was another goblin on
a pogo stick, wearing a pair of heart-
patterned pajamas and a curly blond
wig that bounced around as he jumped.
A third goblin was wobbling along on

roller blades, wearing an old-fashioned bathing suit and a knitted hat.

"More goblins!" cried Kirsty.

"Look at what that goblin on the pogo stick has on a chain around his neck," Destiny said, glowing with excitement. "It's my harmony key!"

The goblin with the key looked very grumpy. The girls and Destiny fluttered closer to hear what he was saying,

making sure to stay out of sight.

"Stop telling me what to do!" he whined to the other goblins. "I'll hide the key later — right now I want to play with my pogo stick!"

"But where are we going to hide it?" demanded another goblin. "We've been all over the store looking for the perfect hiding place, and all we've found are those pesky human girls!"

As the goblins argued, Rachel leaned over to Kirsty and Destiny.

"I think I could get close enough to unfasten the chain from his neck and fly away with it," she whispered.

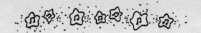

"Oh, be careful!" said Destiny anxiously.

Rachel flew up behind the goblin, ducking down behind his shoulders so that the other goblins couldn't see her. She reached up to unfasten the chain, but one of her wings accidentally brushed against his green skin.

"Something's tickling my neck!" he exclaimed, whirling around. "Hey! A fairy is trying to steal the key!"

He yanked the chain from around

his neck and tucked the key inside his pajama pocket.

"Run away!" bellowed the goblin on roller blades.

The three goblins zoomed into the next department, and Destiny and the girls flew after them. They stopped abruptly just inside the entrance. The department was full of kids . . . and they were the same size as the goblins!

"It's the toy department!" Rachel groaned. "How are we ever going to find three little goblins in here? They look just like children!"

"Let's fly up to the ceiling for a better view," suggested Destiny.

They fluttered up to the ceiling of the toy department. There were crowds of children gathered around low tables piled high with toys. But there was no sign of the goblins.

"It's no use." Destiny sighed. "We'll never find them!"

Suddenly, there was a familiar shriek from the other side of the room.

"That's a goblin!" Rachel exclaimed.

They flew toward the sound, being careful to stay out of sight, and saw the three goblins staring in fear at a guide dog. It was a gentle golden retriever and it wasn't paying much attention to the goblins, but their knobbly green knees were knocking together.

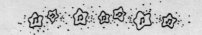

"Help!" squealed the goblin in the blond wig. "It's huge!" He leaped into the arms of the second goblin.

"I don't like hairy monsters, either!" squeaked the second goblin, leaping into the arms of the third goblin, who shrieked and collapsed under their weight.

"Those silly goblins!" said Rachel as the dog and his owner walked away. "Guide dogs are the nicest dogs in the world."

Destiny giggled, but Kirsty was looking thoughtful.

"If they're that scared of dogs, maybe there's another way to get the harmony key back," she said. "Did you notice those battery-powered toy dogs when we came in?"

"Yes," said Rachel eagerly. "They're

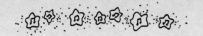

in a wooden pen in the middle of the department."

"Maybe we could trick the goblins into thinking the toy dogs are real!" said Kirsty.

"Then they might forget all about the harmony key once they get spooked by the dogs," said Destiny. "Kirsty, that's a great idea!"

Scaredy-Goblins!

"Let's each go after one goblin," said Rachel. "We can try to drive them toward the pen."

"But what about the kids in the department?" Kirsty asked. "We can't let them see us."

"I can use my magic to distract them for a few minutes," Destiny suggested.

She waved her wand, and a cloud of
magic sparkles danced through the air.
With a series of popping sounds, they
turned into hundreds of multi-colored
balloons. A sparkly banner appeared on
the other side of the department. It read:
FREE BALLOONS!

Shouts of
delight went
up from the
kids as they
ran toward
the beautiful
balloons.
Within
seconds, the
area around

the toy dog pen was completely deserted.

The plan worked perfectly. By

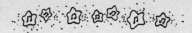

zooming up and down the now empty
aisles of toys, the girls chased the goblins
closer and closer to the wooden pen. At
last they all charged forward and the
goblins collided with
a big CRASH!
They tumbled
head over
heels—
straight
into the
wooden
pen!

The
goblins sat
up and shook their
heads dizzily before realizing they were
surrounded by yapping, flipping dogs.

"EEEK!" squealed the blond-wigged

goblin, trying to
clamber on top
of the second
goblin. "There
are hairy
monsters
everywhere!"

"Help!"
cried the third
goblin, "Save
me!"

"Get off!" wailed the second goblin.

"Goblins!" interrupted Destiny,
hovering above the pen. "I want you to
return the harmony key right now."

"No way!" squeaked the smallest
goblin.

Just at that moment, one of the toy
dogs yapped loudly and flipped over,

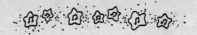

landing on the lap of one of the goblins.

"I think I'm going to faint!" the goblin whimpered.

"If you give me the key, I'll make sure you're all safe from these monsters," said Destiny, folding her arms.

"Just give her the key!" The goblin trembled. "I don't want to get eaten!"

The blond-wigged goblin pulled the harmony key out of his pocket and threw it to Destiny, who shrank it down to fairy-size in midair and

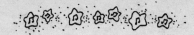

caught it in one hand.

"Those 'monsters' are just toys!" she said, rising high into the air. "Now you have to stop causing so much trouble and leave the store!"

"What?" roared the smallest goblin. "You pesky fairies!"

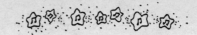

"This is your fault!" shouted the third goblin to the one with the blond wig. "You and that silly pogo stick!"

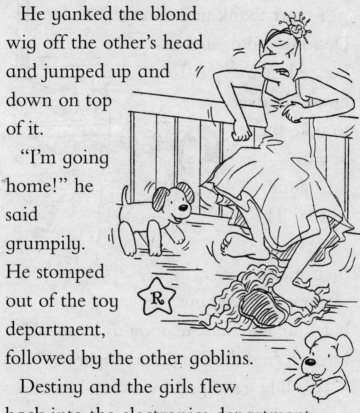

He yanked the blond wig off the other's head and jumped up and down on top of it.

"I'm going home!" he said grumpily. He stomped out of the toy department, followed by the other goblins.

Destiny and the girls flew back into the electronics department next to the TV screens. They were so

excited that they had outsmarted the
goblins and gotten the harmony key
back!

"I can't thank you enough,"
Destiny said as she
hugged them
both. "I have
to take the
key to
Fairyland
so that The
Angels get
their music back
in time for the show,
but I'll come back as soon as I can. We
have to find the magic microphone!"

"We'll be ready and waiting," Rachel
promised.

Destiny smiled and waved her wand over the girls, returning them to human size. Then she disappeared in a shower of glitter and music notes.

After a few seconds, there was a golden crackle and a picture of The Angels appeared on the television screens. They were laughing and hugging.

"Found in the nick of time!" Emilia declared, waving a book of sheet music in the air.

The girls smiled happily at each other as the picture faded. Then Rachel glanced at the clock on the wall and gasped.

"Kirsty, there are only four more hours until the charity concert!" she exclaimed.

Kirsty's eyes widened, and she clapped a hand over her mouth in surprise. "Oh, Rachel, if we can't find the magic microphone, Jack Frost could still ruin the concert for everyone by making the sound and lighting systems go haywire," she said.

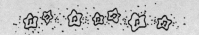

"Don't worry, Kirsty. I'm sure we'll find the magic microphone in time," Rachel said. "After all, we've got Destiny to help us. If anyone can find it, we can!"

The Magic Microphone

Contents

The Return of Jack Frost

Rachel and Kirsty's thoughts raced as
they got changed. They had to get ready
for the Christmas lights ceremony and
The Angels' charity concert. They felt
excited and worried at the same time.
Jack Frost had already tried to ruin
things by stealing Destiny the Rock Star
Fairy's three magic objects. Even though
the girls had gotten back the sparkly
sash and the harmony key, the magic

microphone was still missing. Some sort
of technical glitch could still mess up the
concert!

"Look at the stars twinkling in the
sky," said Kirsty, pressing her nose
against the hotel-room window and
gazing up. "It's a beautiful night."

"I'm glad," said Rachel, joining her at
the window. "The Christmas lighting
ceremony would get canceled if it
rained!"

"Hurry up, girls!" called Mrs. Tate from outside their room. "The Angels will be here soon."

Kirsty looked at the clock on the wall. "Oh, Rachel, it's almost time," she said. "And there's still no sign of the magic microphone!"

"I know," said Rachel, looking serious, "but I'm sure we'll find it. We can't let Jack Frost ruin things by making us worry. Just think, Kirsty: Tonight we'll be helping The Angels turn on the city's Christmas lights! Can you believe it?"

"No!" said Kirsty, grinning at her best friend. "I've seen it on TV so many times, but it just doesn't seem real that we're going to be part of it!"

"Come on, girls!" called Mrs. Tate again.

Rachel and Kirsty smiled at each other in excitement, then pulled on their coats and hurried out of their room.

The Angels were waiting for the girls downstairs in the hotel lobby. They waved when they saw Rachel and Kirsty.

"Have a wonderful time, girls," said Mrs. Walker, kissing them both. "We'll see you later, after the ceremony!"

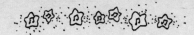

Their parents left to make their own way to Main Street, and Rachel and Kirsty rushed over to The Angels.

"Girls, you look great!" said Serena, giving them each a hug. "Come on, our car's here!"

They led the girls out of the hotel. A long, pink Cadillac was waiting outside, with a smiling chauffeur behind the wheel.

Feeling like rock stars themselves, Rachel and Kirsty climbed in and snuggled into the soft, cream-colored seats. The Angels joined them, and then the Cadillac purred away.

"We're really excited about turning on the lights," Emilia told them. "It's such a special occasion."

"Lots of people get really dressed up, and there's a great party atmosphere," Lexy added eagerly. "It's almost like a carnival!"

118

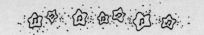

Serena laughed and pointed at a scooter that was riding alongside them in traffic.

"See what we mean?" she giggled.

Kirsty and Rachel looked over at the scooter, and their mouths fell open in surprise. Six goblins were standing on the back of the bike in a pyramid, just like stunt riders! They were waving their arms around to try to keep their balance, looking very unsteady and nervous.

"Oh, no!" groaned Kirsty in a low voice. "Rachel,

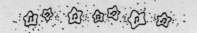

look at the driver!"

Spikes of silvery blue icicles were poking out from underneath the driver's helmet. It was Jack Frost!

As Rachel clutched Kirsty's arm in alarm, Jack Frost turned and gave them a horrible, mocking smile. Then he held up a glittering gold object. "The magic microphone!" whispered Rachel in Kirsty's ear. "And there's no way we can get to it!"

"If only Destiny were here," Kirsty said.

With a final flourish of the microphone and a cackling laugh, Jack Frost picked up speed and roared away. He sped in and out of the busy traffic,

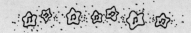

with the goblins clinging on for dear life.

Suddenly, the goblin at the top wobbled. He flapped his arms like crazy, looking like he was trying to fly, but it was no use. As the girls watched in horror, he lost his balance, fell off the scooter, and landed right in the middle of the busy road!

Destiny to the Rescue!

The goblin leaped to his feet as quickly as he could, but the scooter was already almost out of sight. Furious, the goblin jumped up and down in the middle of the road and shook his fist after the disappearing pyramid of goblins.

"It's lucky that everyone wears special outfits for the ceremony," said Kirsty in a low voice. "People will think he's in a costume."

Car horns honked at the angry goblin, and he shook his fist at them, too. Then he spotted a bus and jumped on board. The girls saw him slump down into a seat, folding his arms and looking very grumpy.

Luckily, The Angels hadn't noticed anything. They were practicing their harmonies for the concert that evening, and the car was filled with their sweet, clear voices. Normally, Kirsty and Rachel would have been thrilled to hear this private performance, but right now they were just worried about the magic microphone.

"We have to tell Destiny that Jack Frost is here," Rachel whispered in Kirsty's ear.

"I know," said Kirsty. "But how? She can't appear to us now, because The Angels would see her."

Suddenly, the soft purr of the Cadillac's engine was replaced by a banging, rattling sound. The car began to jerk and shudder, and then it came to a stop in the middle of the road.

The Angels stopped singing and looked around in alarm.

"That doesn't sound good," said Lexy.

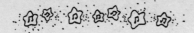

"We're going to be late for the ceremony!" Serena cried.

The chauffeur got out and opened the hood. A cloud of steam hissed, and he coughed and waved his hand to clear the air.

"Let's go and see if we can help," said Emilia. "Girls, you stay here. Hopefully this won't take long!"

The Angels got out of the car and
joined the chauffeur as he peered at the
engine. With the hood lifted, neither the
Angels nor the chauffeur could see into
the car, which was lucky, because . . .

"Oh, Kirsty, look!" Rachel cried in
excitement.

The gear stick was glowing and
sparkling. Then, with a burst of tiny
fireworks in the shape of music notes,
the top of it flipped open like a lid. A
platform rose out of it
with Destiny right
in the middle!

"Destiny!" cried
Rachel and Kirsty
together.

"Hi, girls!"
said the fairy.

She gave them a dazzling smile.

"Jack Frost is here in the human world!" Kirsty blurted out, her words tumbling over themselves.

"Oh, no!" Destiny exclaimed. "How do you know?"

The girls explained what they had seen.

"We have to follow him!" cried Destiny at once.

"Yes, but right now we're not going anywhere," said Rachel, waving her arm toward the open hood. "The car broke down!"

"The Angels are supposed to be turning on the Christmas lights very soon," Kirsty added urgently. "If they can't get there, the ceremony will be ruined!"

"This is all because the magic microphone is still missing," Destiny said with a frown. "You see, it keeps things working smoothly around rock stars, but in the wrong hands it could make all sorts of technical things go wrong. That could mean failing sound equipment, mixed-up lighting . . ."

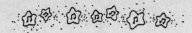

"Or broken car engines?" Rachel finished.

"Exactly," Destiny said, nodding. "But I can fix that!"

She flew over and landed delicately on Rachel's shoulder. Then she waved her wand at the front of the car, and a healthy roar came from the engine.

"Hurray!" cried Rachel and Kirsty, clapping their hands together.

Destiny quickly hid inside Rachel's bag.

Looking very relieved, The Angels and the chauffeur

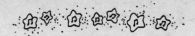

jumped back into the car, and they
continued on their way again. Rachel
and Kirsty watched the clock anxiously.
Could they reach Main Street in time
for the ceremony?

City of Surprises

The car arrived at Main Street with
only a minute to spare, and The Angels
and Rachel and Kirsty jumped out and
hurried up the steps to the podium. The
waiting crowds cheered, and the mayor
smiled in relief.

"Keep a lookout for Jack Frost!"
said Destiny, peeking out of the top of
Rachel's bag.

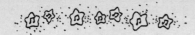

Rachel and Kirsty didn't need to be told to do that! Their eyes were already scanning the packed crowd, searching for any sign of Jack Frost's spiky head.

The Angels stood in the middle of the stage and waved to their fans. Next to a microphone was the big red button that would turn on the Christmas lights.

"We are thrilled to have been asked to turn on the city's Christmas lights this year," Serena began. "It's such an honor to . . ."

As she continued her speech, Kirsty

gripped Rachel's hand tightly.

"I see him!" she exclaimed.

Jack Frost was standing at the edge of the crowd. Before the girls could think of what to do, he stuck out his tongue and then tapped his wand against the magic microphone.

Immediately, the streetlights and all the lights in the stores went out. Main Street was plunged into darkness! Gasps went up from the crowd, and the girls heard the mayor stumbling around the stage. He tapped the microphone, but it wasn't working.

"Don't panic!" he shouted as loudly

as he could. "Everyone, stay where you are! Just a technical glitch, that's all!" He turned to his assistant and added in a low voice, "Find out what's wrong and fix it—quickly!"

Destiny flew out of Rachel's bag.

"Don't move," she said. "I'm going to turn you into fairies!"

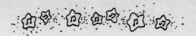

The girls couldn't see her wand, but
they could feel themselves shrinking
down to fairy-size as filmy wings grew
on their backs.

"Take my hands," Destiny whispered.

Rachel and Kirsty stretched out their
hands in the darkness, and felt Destiny's
fingers intertwine with theirs. Then they
fluttered their wings, rose into the air,
and flew to where they had last seen
Jack Frost standing.

When they left Main Street, they saw that the lights were still on in the side streets. Almost at once, Rachel spotted a skinny green leg disappearing through the stage door of a nearby theater.

"In there!" she cried.

The girls raced toward the door and zipped into the theater.

Inside, the lights were down and a musical was in full swing. The girls paused in dismay. The loud singing was drowning out any sound of giggling goblins that they might have followed. They had to shout to even hear each other.

"Let's fly over the rows one by one and search," Kirsty yelled.

They split up and began a careful search of the theater, from the front to the back. No one saw them because it was so dark, and all  eyes were on the stage. Just as the song finished, Kirsty grabbed the others' hands and pointed. Jack Frost was sitting in the very back row with five goblins!

They all had large bags of candy or popcorn open on their laps, and their feet were resting on the backs of the seats in front of them.

They were making so much noise that they were disturbing everyone around them. The goblins were noisily unwrapping candy and making sucking sounds as they shoved them into their mouths. Jack Frost was heckling the actors by shouting "Boo!" as he helped himself to the goblins' treats. The goblins hadn't quite grasped the idea of heckling,

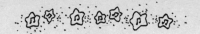

though. One just kept yelling "Rhubarb!" Another was shouting, "Heckle! Heckle!" and the remaining three were crying, "It's behind you!" at the actors. "Those awful troublemakers!" cried Destiny in distress. "They're ruining the show for everyone!"

Musical Mayhem

"They haven't seen us yet," said Kirsty. "Let's creep up on them and try to find the magic microphone without them noticing."

"Good idea," said Rachel. "They must think they've lost us."

They flew carefully toward the back row. Closer . . . closer . . . until at last they were right behind Jack Frost's seat.

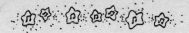

"Look!" whispered Destiny.

Underneath his seat, lit up by the pale aisle lights, was the shining magic microphone!

"All we have to do is reach out and take it," said Rachel breathlessly.

Slowly and quietly, the three friends stretched their hands toward the microphone . . . but then they heard a

nasty chuckle above them. Jack Frost was peering over the back of his seat—and pointing his wand at them! "Oh, I don't think so, little fairies!" he

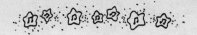

cackled. "You'll never get the better
of me!"

Kirsty opened her mouth to respond,
but she never got the chance. The doors
of the theater crashed open and revealed
a wet, muddy green figure wearing a
bike helmet.

"YOU LEFT ME BEHIND!" he
bellowed.

It was the goblin who had fallen off the
scooter! He was covered
in mud, dripping
with water, and
boiling with
rage as he
pointed a bony
finger at the
other goblins.

"I got thrown

off the bus because I didn't have a ticket," he screeched. "I was pushed into muddy puddles, squashed by late-night shoppers, and almost trampled by a police horse, and it's *all your fault!*"

He flung himself at the other goblins, and the back row suddenly became a mess of green arms and legs. Squeals and yells filled the air.

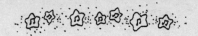

Jack Frost hadn't taken his eyes off the girls. He wasn't going to let them take the magic microphone while his back was turned! But because his attention was on Rachel, Kirsty, and Destiny, he didn't see the angry faces of the people in the row in front, turning around to glare at him. He also didn't see them get out of their seats to call the ushers over. He definitely didn't see the ushers arriving and reaching out to grab the goblins and their master!

"Hey!" yelled Jack Frost as an usher grabbed him, pinning his arms to his sides.

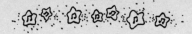

"Let go of me!"
wailed the muddy,
screeching goblin
as another usher
seized him by
the shoulders.

The goblins
and Jack Frost
writhed and
yelled, but the ushers
held them firmly.

"I don't care how much effort you've
put into these silly costumes," whispered
the head usher furiously. "We're not
putting up with this noise a minute
longer. We're removing you from the
theater!"

Jack Frost turned toward the girls, who
had ducked out of sight. He struggled

to get his wand arm free so that he
could cast an icy spell, but the usher was
bigger than him. Three ushers marched
out of the theater with an angry,
kicking goblin under each arm. They
were led by the head usher holding Jack
Frost in an iron grip.

"You'll regret
this!" Jack Frost
bellowed.

His wails
faded away
as he and
the goblins
were thrown
out of the
building, and

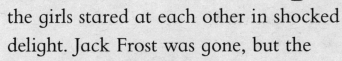

the girls stared at each other in shocked
delight. Jack Frost was gone, but the

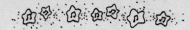

magic microphone was still under the seat! They could hardly believe their good luck.

Destiny waved her wand, and a rush of glittering fairy dust returned the magic microphone to her hands and to its Fairyland size. Not a moment too soon, either!

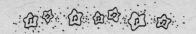

"Hurry!" said Kirsty, fluttering her wings and rising into the air. She grinned. "Let's get back to Main Street as fast as we can. We have to save the ceremony!"

The Christmas Concert

A minute later, Rachel and Kirsty
landed back behind the podium on
Main Street, next to The Angels. The
technicians were still trying to fix the
lights, and the crowd was starting to
grumble.

Destiny flung her arms around the girls.

"I can never thank you enough for helping me!" she said, her voice bubbling with happiness. "Everything will be all right for The Angels and the charity concert now. I must hurry back to Fairyland to return the magic microphone—and get ready for my own concert!"

With a sprinkle of fairy dust, Destiny returned the girls to their normal size.

"I'll see you again soon!" Destiny whispered in their ears.

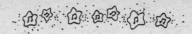

"Good-bye!" they whispered back.

Then she was gone. Seconds later, all the lights came back on. The crowd cheered and laughed, as Rachel and Kirsty blinked and looked around.

"A little bit of drama adds to the fun!" joked Emilia, stepping up to the microphone to speak. Serena, Lexy, Rachel, and Kirsty joined her in front of the microphone and put their hands over the big red button. "Ladies and gentlemen, girls and boys, all we really want to say is . . ."

"Merry Christmas, everyone!" they shouted together.

They all pressed the button, and the Christmas lights burst into life, illuminating Main Street and filling every corner with color and light. As the crowd cheered, The Angels  were whisked away to get ready for their concert. The girls' parents were waiting next to the limousine that would take them all to the Supersonic Stadium.

When they arrived at the stadium a few
minutes later, the audience was buzzing
with anticipation. Kirsty and Rachel felt
their hearts thumping with excitement as
they took their seats in the VIP area and
waited for the performance to begin.

It was a spectacular concert. The
audience was dancing in the aisles after
the first song, and when The Angels sang
their biggest hit, the cheers and screams

were so loud that the girls could hardly hear the song! But the real highlight of the show was their new charity single, "Key to My Heart."

At the end of the concert, Rachel and Kirsty went backstage to say good-bye to The Angels and thank them for a wonderful couple of days. After they had hugged Emilia, Lexy, and Serena, the girls and their parents stepped into the waiting limousine for the last time.

Rachel and Kirsty couldn't get the catchy new song out of their heads, and they sang it all the way back to the hotel.

"You're always there to hold my hand.
You stand by me, you understand.
When I'm with you I feel so glad,
The truest friend I ever had.
I know we two will never part,
And that's the real key to my heart!"

"I'm so sleepy!" said Rachel with a big yawn as they changed into their pajamas in the hotel room.

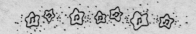

"Me, too," said Kirsty, throwing back the covers to climb into bed. "Oh, Rachel—look!"

On her pillow was a beautiful silver hand mirror.

"I've got one, too!" cried Rachel.

The girls picked up the mirrors and turned them over. On the back of each one was a delicate inscription that read, *With love and thanks, Destiny xoxo*. They turned them over again and gasped with delight. When they looked into the glass, they could see Destiny waving at them, with King Oberon and Queen Titania behind her.

"Thank you, Rachel and Kirsty!" Destiny said. "The concert was a wonderful success and it's all thanks to you!"

"We're so glad!" Rachel whispered. "Good night, everyone! We hope to see you again soon!"

The girls snuggled down into their beds and smiled sleepily at each other.

"We've had lots of exciting, magical adventures," murmured Kirsty. "But you know what, Rachel? I think that this has definitely been the most star-studded one yet!"

SPECIAL EDITION

There's another fairy adventure
just around the corner! Join Rachel
and Kirsty as they help

Paige the
Christmas Play Fairy!

Read on for a special sneak peek . .

Paige Appears

Mr. Robinson turned in surprise. "Who are you, my dear?" he asked.

"Kirsty Tate," replied Kirsty. "I'm Rachel's friend, and I'm staying with her until Christmas Eve."

"I can teach Kirsty the dance steps," Rachel added quickly.

"And I'll practice every single minute

until the show!" said Kirsty.

"Well, that solves our problem!"
Mr. Robinson said, looking delighted.
"Thank you so much!" He glanced at
Kirsty. "You look about the same size
as Clarissa. Why don't you try on her
costume and see if it fits?" Then he
hurried off.

When Kirsty opened the door of the
dressing room, it was dark inside. Rachel
flicked on the light switch. Instantly, a
mirror surrounded by light bulbs filled
the room with a dazzling white light.
A second later, one of the bulbs popped
loudly and went out. The noise made
Rachel and Kirsty jump.

"Rachel, look!" Kirsty gasped.

Sparkling gold fairy dust had burst
from the broken bulb. As the dust

cleared, Rachel and Kirsty saw a pretty little fairy dancing in the air in front of them!

"Hello," the fairy called. "I'm Paige the Christmas Play Fairy!"

RAINBOW magic™

There's Magic in Every Series!

The Rainbow Fairies
The Weather Fairies
The Jewel Fairies
The Pet Fairies
The Fun Day Fairies
The Petal Fairies
The Dance Fairies
The Music Fairies
The Sports Fairies
The Party Fairies
The Ocean Fairies
The Night Fairies

Read them all!

■ SCHOLASTIC

www.scholastic.com
www.rainbowmagiconline.com

HIT entertainment

RMFAIR